Francis Discovers Possible

Words by
Ashlee Latimer

Pictures by
Shahrzad Maydani

ABRAMS BOOKS FOR YOUNG READERS
NEW YORK

Francis loved words.

She loved words, and she loved Tuesdays.

At Francis's school, Tuesdays were word days, and that made Tuesdays the best.

Every week, Francis's teacher, Mr. Prewett, picked one student and let them choose a letter. Their job was to find new words that began with their letter, to share with the class.

This week, it was Francis's turn,
and she had picked the letter **P**.

But first, Mr. Prewett wanted to review
the letters they'd already learned.

"**A** is for **antelope**," Mr. Prewett started.

"**R** is for **rainbow**," Robert said.

"**T** is for **trampoline**!" cried Calliope.

"**E** is for . . ." prompted Mr. Prewett.

"**Elephant**!" shouted Xiomara.

"**Elevator**?" suggested Ekele.

"**Excellent**!" Mr. Prewett winked. "What about **F**?"

"**Frog**!" yelled Sameerah.

"**Fat**—" whispered Tabitha.

"—like Francis," snickered Jericho, loud enough for everyone to hear.

Fat was usually a warm word.
Like belly rubs for Francis's puppy.

Or how her giggles felt too big for
her mouth during hide-and-seek.

Or like cuddling up to read
a book with Mama and using Mama's
fluffy arm as the best pillow.

Tabitha made **Fat** cold. Like the time a hole split Francis's boots and let the puddles inside.

Jericho made Francis feel small, like the time she tripped at recess during tag, and everyone laughed.

Mr. Prewett told Jericho and Tabitha to apologize and offered to jump to Francis's turn to talk.

But Francis didn't want to stand in front of everybody now.

She'd started thinking about **Fat**, and she couldn't seem to stop.

She thought about **Fat** at lunch.

She thought about **Fat** at naptime.

She thought about **Fat** when
Baba picked her up after school.

"How was class today? Did you tell everyone
about pumpernickel and pudding and porcupines?"
Baba asked as he gave Francis a hug.

Francis shook her head against
Baba's soft belly.

"No? Why not?"

Francis wasn't sure what to say.
She didn't want Baba to know **Fat** was bad.

Francis and Baba were both quiet
on their walk to the car.

"Francis," Baba said, after they buckled up,
"I need some fresh air. Could we go to the park?"

Francis considered.

The park was good for thinking.

"Ok, Baba," Francis said.

When Francis and Baba got to the park, he made
a beeline for the swings—their favorite spot—but
Francis didn't want to pump her legs today.

She sat on the closest bench instead.

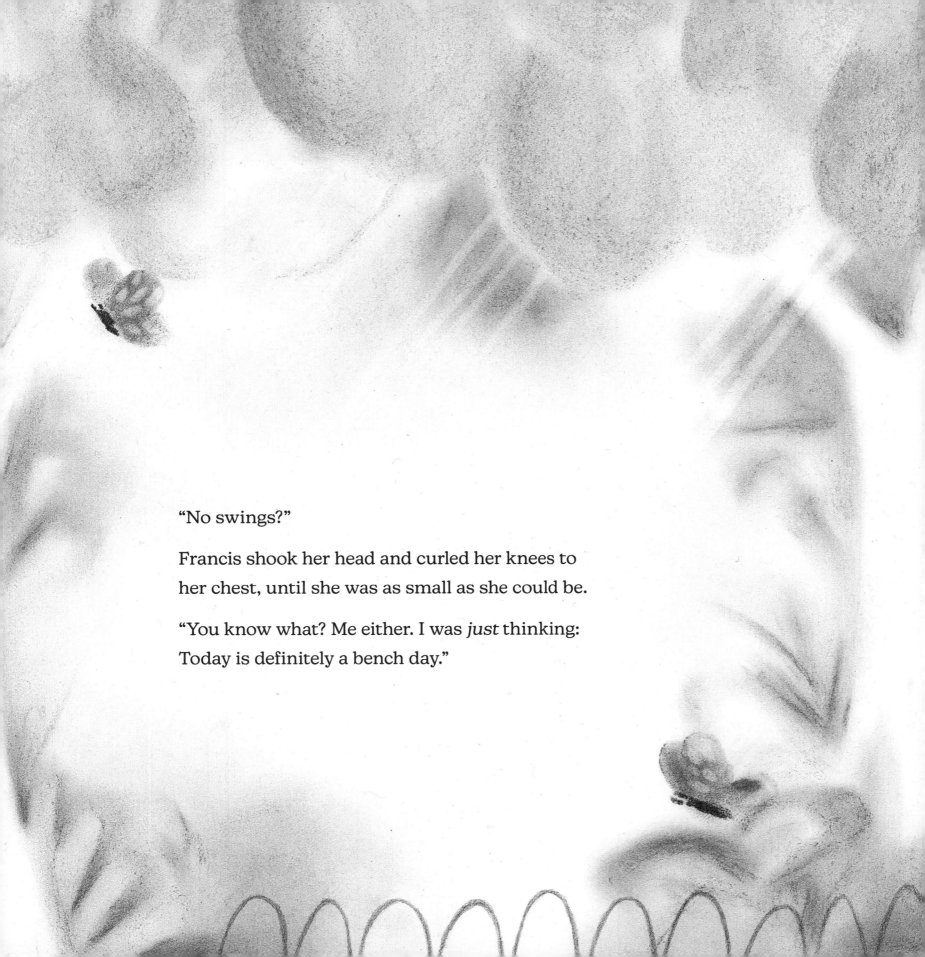

"No swings?"

Francis shook her head and curled her knees to her chest, until she was as small as she could be.

"You know what? Me either. I was *just* thinking: Today is definitely a bench day."

Baba and Francis settled in. It was quiet on the bench.

Then Baba said, "You know Francis,
the Weather Channel thinks it's possible
we'll get snow before—"

Francis's ears perked up.

Possible.

Francis knew so many **P** words,
but this one felt brand-new.

"Baba?" Francis said.

"Mhm?"

"What does the word **Possible** mean?"

Baba tilted his head to the side. "Hmm. What do you think?"

Francis shrugged.

"Maybe . . . **Possible** is something like exploring," Baba suggested.

Then, he held out his hand and whispered, "Why don't we go find out?"

Francis wasn't sure, but she was curious, so she put her hand in Baba's, and off they went.

Was **Possible** like airplanes,
hovering in the sky?

Could **Possible** be like learning to swim? Was it when you held your breath and jumped?

Or did **Possible** look like planting,
and how it takes a long time to grow?

Maybe **Possible** *slap, slap, slapped* like double Dutch
and kept you on your toes!

Francis thought that **Possible** would be one thing, but suddenly it seemed like lots of things.

There was **Possible** in dandelions
and in scooping air into your lungs for a wish!

Possible in puppies, in the squishes of their tummies
and how they're always ready to play.

Possible, like the wind,
dancing leaves to a new place.

Possible made Francis feel warm and big—like **Fat**, before Tabitha made it cold and Jericho made it small.

Possible made her want to take up space and share her words, and wish and dance and play.

Because if puppies and wishes could be **Possible**, maybe Francis was **Possible**, too.

Francis reached up and tugged on Baba's sleeve.

"Baba, I think I'm ready for the swings," said Francis.

And she was.

Author's Note

I grew up a poor, skinny, unpopular white kid in a single-parent household, and almost every book I read as a child reflected some part of my own story back to me in the main characters. But as I got older and my body grew with me, I often didn't see myself in the books I read or movies I watched. If I did, it was usually as a joke or, at best, a plucky best friend. It took years for me to learn to accept my body and see myself as someone who could still be the protagonist of a story—and to begin to write those stories myself.

The character of Francis was born out of my desire for kids of all body types to see, at an early age, fat characters portrayed as people worthy of taking up space in stories—in everyday scenarios and the biggest dreams we can imagine. I was also eager to portray a fat parent who is positive, supportive, and reassuring to their fat child in subtle ways, because I know firsthand the hurt that can occur when self-esteem issues are passed down from parent to child.

Finally, it was important to me to give Francis quiet permission to sit with her emotions when she is confronted with bullying, while allowing her space to find her way through those tough feelings and into a place of possibility. I hope that Francis helps readers discover the same sense of possibility for themselves.

For Zack and the village,
who helped me discover possible
—A.L.

For Rumi and Tisa
—S.M.

The art for this book was created using soft pastels and watercolor.

Cataloging-in-Publication Data has been applied for and may be obtained from the Library of Congress.

ISBN 978-1-4197-4910-0

Text © 2022 Ashlee Latimer
Illustrations © 2022 Shahrzad Maydani
Book design by Heather Kelly

Printed and bound in China
10 9 8 7 6 5 4 3 2 1

Abrams Books for Young Readers are available at special discounts when purchased in quantity for
premiums and promotions as well as fundraising or educational use. Special editions can also be created to specification.
For details, contact specialsales@abramsbooks.com or the address below.

Abrams® is a registered trademark of Harry N. Abrams, Inc.

ABRAMS The Art of Books
195 Broadway, New York, NY 10007
abramsbooks.com